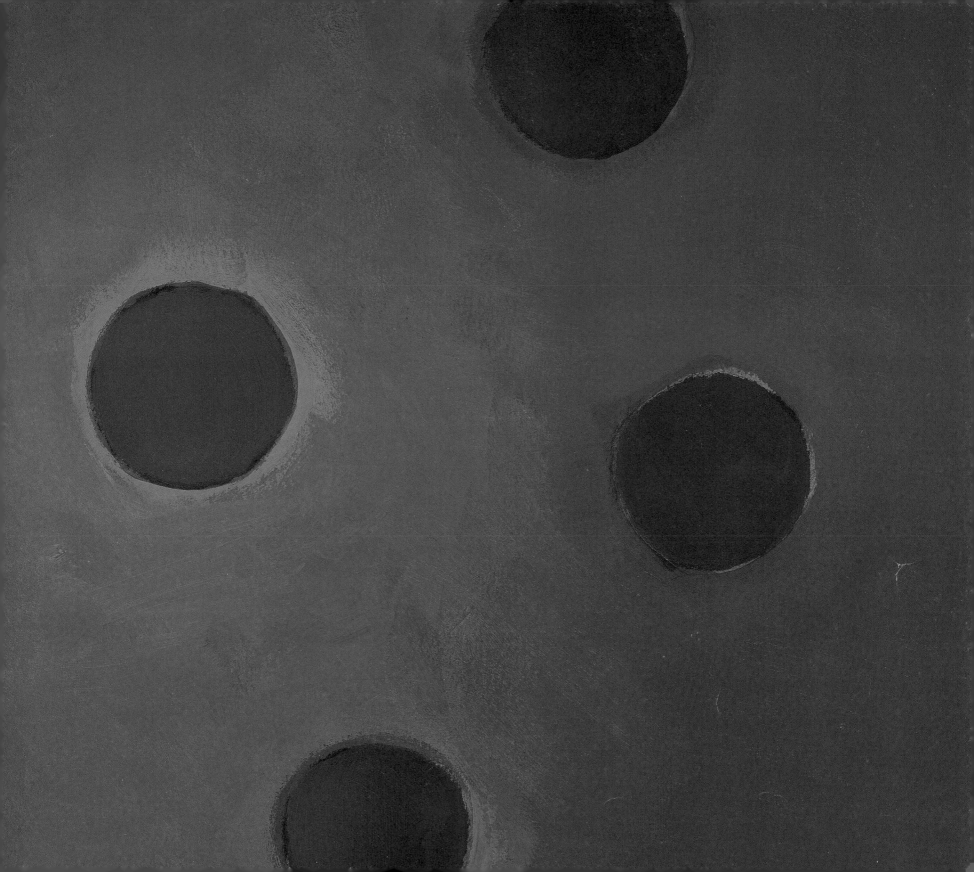

For Andrea & Claudia
— I.F.

For Mum & Dad, who helped
— J.T.

The Very Lazy Ladybird

by Isobel Finn & Jack Tickle

This is the story of
a very lazy ladybird.

She liked to sleep all day . . .

And because she slept
all day and all night,
this lazy ladybird didn't
know how to fly.

One day the lazy
ladybird wanted to
sleep somewhere else.
But what could she do
if she couldn't fly?

Then the lazy
ladybird had
a very good
idea.

"I can't sleep in here,"
cried the lazy ladybird.
"It's far too bumpy."

So when a tiger padded by . . .

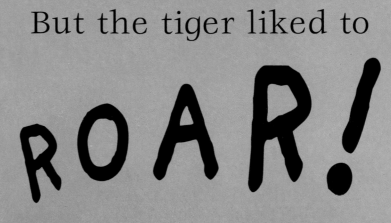

But the tiger liked to

ROAR!

"I can't sleep here,"
said the lazy ladybird.
"It's far too noisy."

So when a crocodile swam by . . .

she hopped on to his tail.

But the crocodile liked to

SWISH

his tail in the water.

"I can't sleep here,"
said the lazy ladybird.
"I'll fall into the river!"

So when a monkey swung by . . .

she hopped on to her head.

But the monkey liked to

SWING

from branch to branch.

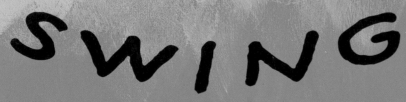

"I can't sleep here," said the lazy ladybird. "I'm feeling dizzy."

So when a bear ambled by . . .

she hopped on to his ear.

But the bear liked to

SCRATCH!

"I can't sleep here," said the lazy ladybird. "He'll never sit still."

So when a tortoise plodded by . . .

she hopped on to her shell.

But the tortoise liked to
S N O O Z E
in the sun.
"I can't sleep here,"
said the lazy ladybird.
"It's far too hot."

So when an elephant trundled by . . .

she hopped on to his trunk.

"At last!" thought the lazy ladybird. "I've found someone who doesn't . . .

jump . . .

But at that very moment . . .

the elephant **sneezed!**

AA

ACHOOo

And poor old lazy ladybird . . .

had to fly at last!

Now **flip** the book to read

The Crunching Munching Caterpillar

Now **flip**
the book to read

The Very
Lazy Ladybird

This edition produced 2005 for
Scholastic Book Clubs and Scholastic Book Fairs
by Little Tiger Press
An imprint of Magi Publications
1 The Coda Centre, 189 Munster Road, London SW6 6AW
www.littletigerpress.com

The Crunching Munching Caterpillar
First published in Great Britain 2000 by Little Tiger Press
Text copyright © Sheridan Cain 2000 • Illustrations copyright © Jack Tickle 2000

The Very Lazy Ladybird
First published in Great Britain 1999 by Little Tiger Press
Text copyright © Isobel Finn 1999 • Illustrations copyright © Jack Tickle 1999

The authors and illustrators have asserted their moral rights.

Printed in Singapore
All rights reserved

ISBN 1 84506 359 7
1 2 3 4 5 6 7 8 9 10

"Wow!" said Young Butterfly. "I'm flying! I'm really flying!"

and a breeze lifted
Caterpillar into the air.

He was no longer
short and plump.
He had WINGS!
Great, big, wonderful
BUTTERFLY WINGS!

When Caterpillar woke up he felt
the warmth of the spring sun.
He was stiff from his long sleep,
but he did not feel very hungry.
He stretched and stretched . . .

He dreamed he was as light as a feather, floating on the breeze.

He dreamed he was a dandelion clock, drifting towards the sun.

He dreamed he had wings and was soaring up in the blue sky above the tall trees . . .

Caterpillar slept all through the winter,
and his sleep was filled with dreams.

Butterfly was right. Caterpillar suddenly felt very sleepy. As Butterfly flew off into the night sky, he fell into a deep, deep sleep.

Butterfly landed gracefully beside him.
"Oh, I wish I could fly like you," sighed Caterpillar.
"But I'm too fat and I have legs instead of wings."
Butterfly smiled a secret, knowing smile.
"Who knows? Perhaps one day you will fly,
light as a feather, like me," she said.
"But now, little Caterpillar, you should
go to sleep. You look very tired."

He wrapped a leaf around himself to keep warm.
He was just about to go to sleep when . . .

Caterpillar carried on crunch-munching
all day, until the light began to dim.

Crunch
Munch

Crunch
Munch

"I'd love to fly high in the air like that," said Caterpillar.
"Well, you can't," said Sparrow. "You need to be as light as the dandelion clock that floats on the breeze. You're far too fat to fly. Your legs are for walking."
"I guess so," said Caterpillar glumly.

Sparrow landed
beside him.

Caterpillar was just about to start
his breakfast when . . .

Caterpillar woke to
the sound of twittering.
Birds swooped and soared
in the early morning light.

Bzzzzoommm

Bumblebee flew off to the next bush. Watching Bumblebee fly had made Caterpillar *very* hungry, so he crunched and he munched until it was time for bed.

crunch Munch
crunch Munch
yaw-w-n!

Bumblebee flew up into the air and buzzed busily from flower to flower.

Bzzzzz

Bzzzz

"I'd love to fly like that," said Caterpillar.
"Well, you can't," said Bumblebee.
"I've got wings, and you've got legs. Your legs are for walking."
"I guess so," sighed Caterpillar.

"Wow!" said Caterpillar,
"how did you get here?"
"Simple," said Bumblebee,
"I flew. I have wings. Look!"
"Oh, I'd like some of those,"
said Caterpillar.

Bzzzzzzzzzzzz

Bumblebee landed
beside him!

One day, Caterpillar was about to
crunch into another leaf when . . .

Munch
Munch

crunch
crunch

Caterpillar was always hungry.
For weeks he crunched and munched
his way through the fresh,
juicy leaves of a blackberry bush.

Bzzzzzzzzzz

Sheridan Cain
Jack Tickle

The Crunching Munching Caterpillar

~JT

For Jim and Raechele

~SC

For my family